Michael Ferguson was born in Greenore, Co. Louth, on 4th April 1949; educated in St Michael's College, Omeath, Co. Louth; involved with local drama group since 1984 as an actor and director; commenced writing in 2009 with "Bernadette" – four-act story of Lourdes. Subsequent writings include: "Noah" (one-act comedy), "Oliver Plunkett – The Final Days" (written for and produced by R.T.E.), "A Time to Remember" (1 act, acknowledged by House of Commons motion no. 365, 02/11/2016), "Murder Inspired" (Murder Mystery Night), "Anna – The Girl Who Stood Out in the Cold" and is currently writing a two-act comedy set in Carlingford in 1949, entitled "The Blacksmith".

Dedication

Dedicated to Kublai and Kal-el Ferguson.

Michael Ferguson

ANNA – THE GIRL WHO STOOD OUT IN THE COLD

A PLAY IN TWO ACTS

AUSTIN MACAULEY PUBLISHERS™

LONDON • CAMBRIDGE • NEW YORK • SHARJAH

A CIP catalogue record for this title is available from the British Library.

ISBN 9781788488907 (Paperback)
ISBN 9781788488914 (Hardback)
ISBN 9781788488921 (E-Book)

www.austinmacauley.com

First Published (2018)
Austin Macauley Publishers Ltd™
25 Canada Square
Canary Wharf
London
E14 5LQ

Characters

Rudolf Hoess – Commandant Auschwitz
Hans Friedrich – SS Officer
Franz Munch – SS Officer
Bruno Bettelheim – Kapo
Leopold Kowsky – Kapo
Both Kapos double up as German and Russian soldiers

Inmates

Marysia Jedrzejak – Polish Jew
Therese Steiner – Jew from Guernsey
Helena Citronova – Jehovah's Witness
Ilse Valdeman – Ukrainian Gypsy
Anna Kersten – German Jew
Margot Kersten – Anna's Sister
Henryk Goldszmit – Jewish Orphan
Andrejez Stapor – Jewish Orphan

Act 1, Scene 1

1. Music of *Erika* (German marching song), with film footage of German troops and Hitler in various scenes for the duration of the song.
2. Music of *O Fortuna* from Carmina Burana by Carl Orff, with images of inmates of Auschwitz and if possible, stills of actual cast members superimposed on film.

During the playing of this piece, the women inmates will be herded in from the side entrance of the theatre by the two Kapos and marched across the stage to the other exit, accompanied by shouts and other physical abuse with use of whips and cudgels.

Alternatively, inmates enter at the start of *O Fortuna* and walk incessantly in a circle for the duration of the music, indicating futility and Zombie-like existence, or they enter at the crescendo of *O Fortuna* for a greater impact.

Act 1, Scene 11 – Parade Ground, Auschwitz, January 1943

Act 1, Scene 111 – Women's quarters, Auschwitz/Birkenau, 27 Jan 1945

Two rows of bunk beds angled together with an old-fashioned stove at the centre

INTERVAL

Act 2: Later that night

Act 1, Scene 11

Two German soldiers step on to the stage, one from each side.

Enter Commandant Hoess to the centre stage.

Enter Hans Freidrich and Franz Munch from either side.

Franz: It is a great honour and privilege to have you back at the helm, Herr Commander

Freidrich: May I also add my compliments to your reinstatement? And I am honoured to assist you in the execution of your primary directive from the Fuhrer himself.

Hoess: My dear Hans, your choice of words are, to say the least, prophetic and appropriate with emphasis on the 'execution' of the enormous task ahead of us.

Franz: On my own behalf, Herr Commander, I state under oath that 'my honour lies in loyalty'.

Hoess: I am very pleased to hear these words, gentlemen, and it is a great comfort to have such able-bodied lieutenants to carry out our objectives without question or conscience.

Freidrich: I look forward to using the techniques I experienced on the eastern front. No mercy was given, I assure you, to those sub humans who dared oppose us, so I have no qualms or conscience in terminating the lives of these animals in our care.

Hoess: I am very impressed, Hans, but only time will tell if this great experience is applied efficiently in attaining the work quota assigned to us on a daily basis. And what of you, Franz? What great expertise do you proclaim in achieving the final solution?

Franz: Unlike Lieutenant Freidrich, my expertise is confined to administration duties alone, as I have no first-hand experience of mass executions. However, my skills are of equal importance in ensuring the unhindered transportation of the Jews from all over Europe.

Hoess: Yes, indeed, you have both been highly recommended for your abilities. You, Hans, by none other than Reinhard Heydrich and you, Franz, by Adolf Eichmann so I have no doubt concerning your references.

Let me, however, outline my own levels of expectations and a criteria of character which I expect, no, not expect but demand of every SS man and woman who adorn their uniforms with the distinctive death's head insignia. We must be as hard as granite; otherwise, the work of the Fuhrer will perish.

Don't waste any time on the Jews. It is a joy, finally, to be able to deal with the Jewish race. The more that die the better. Why do they exist, they shouldn't be, they ought to disappear forever. I assure you, gentlemen, that anyone who shows even the slightest vestige of sympathy towards the prisoners must immediately vanish from our ranks. I need only hard, totally committed SS men and women. There is no place amongst us for soft people. What do I care if 10,000 Jewish women and children die while digging an anti-tank ditch? Their deaths are justified. If by digging that ditch, even one German soldier's life is saved, then so be it.

We must not fear criticism of future generations who may brand our deeds as acts of barbarity but we will be vindicated when the world at last recognises our victory over the prisoners of all peoples – International Jewry. Even our good doctors have no problems with the Hippocratic Oath.

And by way of reconciliation, may I quote our very own Dr Klein, 'Because I swore the Hippocratic Oath, I will remove a septic appendix from a human body. The Jews are the septic appendix in the body of the world, that's why they must be removed.'

This then is our primary objective: the elimination of an entire race whose only contribution to society is that they are totally responsible for the ills in that society.

We take great pride that our Nazi party has taken over every aspect of power in Germany. A master race under one leader. Our religion is the Aryan Race and our SS faith will replace Christianity. With this power and with this faith, we will strip the Jewish nation of every facet of humanity. Our tactics have already been proven at Babi Yar where 33,771 men, women and children walked calmly into the valley of death and there they remain for eternity.

I don't know why there are Jews and bacteria and lice and fleas and vermin of all sorts. What I do know is that Judaism must be destroyed, that is my sacred belief. The average life expectancy for your own benefit and knowledge of all inmates is, a Jew, three days, a Catholic priest, two weeks, all others, one month.

There are no rules here in Auschwitz; all Jewish life is worthless. The final solution will come to fruition under Adolf Hitler. For the Fuhrer, we are prepared to commit atrocities. Heil Hitler.

Act 1 – Scene 11, January 1945

Scene opens with 12-year-old Anna sitting, coughing, beside an open stove, with her sister Margot holding her tight. Helena stands to her left, Marysia lies on bed racks looking on; Ilse sits over on the right, holding a Balalaika with no strings. Therese Steiner stands, looking out the window.

Margot: She'll never make it through the night, I tell you. She's frail enough already without facing a night which is 30 degrees below 0.

Anna: I'm afraid, Margot, I'm afraid of the cold and the dark and I am afraid of dying.

Margot: You will not die, you are my only sister and as long as there is a breath left in my body, I will give it to you. Have faith, Anna. God has protected us so far and surely this war must end soon.

Marysia: God, God, don't you dare mention that word God. Let me tell you little girls that God does not exist.

Therese: Shame on you, Marysia, without God there is no hope and without hope there is no life.

Marysia: Did your so-called God hear the screams of the women and children in the gas chambers when the doors were closed and the awful reality of death by crystallised prussic acid, cyanide, choked the life out of them. Did He just close His eye and ears to the suffering or was He so ashamed of His creation that even He chose to deny the existence of this holiday camp called Auschwitz?

Therese: Hopefully, we will never know what it was like to be inside the gas chamber and it is a domain which will elude us forever. It is a morbid fascination but is also a zone of privacy. I like to believe that in that privacy of death, suffering was but momentary and the victims awakened to a reality of incomparable peace and happiness.

Marysia: You are a dreamer, Therese Steiner, or do you deny this reality which faces us all? You think suffering in the gas chamber was but momentary. Let me tell you that I have heard the screams of pain and the cries of despair to a God who chose not to hear them. The screams lasted for fifteen minutes or more, and finally, the last scraping of fingernails on walls and steel doors gave way to a deathly silence. The final ignominy being the laughter of sadistic SS guards who celebrated yet another successful execution.

Margot: My sister is only 12 years old and despite what you say, she will have to stand outside in her bare feet in the snow. There is no one to help her, neither God nor man.

Ilse: Yes, Therese, what heavenly justice prevails when poor Anna is sentenced to stand barefoot throughout a winter's night by a sadistic 20-year-old SS guard just because she failed to meet her work quota?

Therese: This is the reality we must face, Ilse, and if we face it together and firmly believe that whatever the deep heart within you desires, it 'ill come to you through long and winding passages. We face a lonely night ahead but remember that faith is the little bird that sings when the dawn is still dark.

Anna: Therese, you use beautiful words and paint such beautiful pictures and suddenly, I am not afraid anymore. Please help me to believe in God again.

Therese: The reason we are all here is because of God or should I say, because we worship Him under a different uniform with the Star of David as our emblem.

Ilse: I am not here because I am a Jew, no, I am here because I am a gypsy so I am even lower than the Jews as judged by our master race. Even worse, I am a Ukrainian Gypsy.

Helena: I too am a different persuasion and even though I am of the true Aryan race and born in Düsseldorf, I also merit the title outcast because of my belief in Jehovah.

Marysia: So you are a Jehovah's Witness?

Helena: Yes, I am a Jehovah's Witness and I also share Therese's faith and belief that God will deliver us all from this terrible place.

Anna: I beg to report Herr Commander that I am the culprit prisoner, no 967124 (in German).

Ilse: What glimmer of hope have we seen since we came here? There is no laughter and strangely, there are no physical tears either. There are no cries of remorse, only cries of pain and hunger and despair. Tears are not enough to replace that which breached the basic rules of humanity, and why, it's like nature protects us; it takes us away from the reality of our feelings.

Margot: You're right, we cannot expect help from anyone except ourselves, so what can we do to help Anna survive the night?

Therese: I will help her or at least prepare her for the ordeal ahead.

Marysia: I warn you, Therese, do not make any false promises which you can never uphold or fulfil.

Therese: I will make such a promise, Anna. You said earlier that you are not afraid anymore and will believe in God again.

Anna: I remember what you said about hope and will trust in its promise.

Therese: That's right, Anna. And I remind you all once more that hope is faith holding out its hand in the dark.

Hope is not the closing of your eyes to the difficulty, the risk, or the failure. It is a trust that if I fail now, I shall not fail forever. And if I am hurt, I shall be healed, it is a trust that life is good and love is powerful.

Margot: All right, Therese, please help my sister.

Therese: Anna, I spoke earlier about a penny candle. Let me tell you a story about a little boy your age who, in order to gain his father's freedom from slavery, volunteered to stand naked on a mountain top from dusk to dawn, during the depths of winter. The slave owner was sure that the boy would die during the night but was amazed when he survived the ordeal and obtained freedom for his family. How was this possible? A miracle, perhaps? No, you see, on that night, his father lit a bonfire on the opposite mountain top and he told his son to keep looking at the fire and imagine that he was standing right beside it and feeling its warmth. His father kept the fire burning brightly all through the night and his son's gaze never left it. The son survived the ordeal and even claimed later to have felt a physical warmth which to all extents was utterly impossible. Now, I cannot offer you a bonfire but I can offer you a penny candle, which will shine out to you through the window and will radiate not only light but hope and faith and the strongest emotion on earth: love.

(All stunned silence)

Therese: I beg you to believe me, believe in yourselves, believe in the power of good over evil and believe me, Anna will live.

Marysia: This is like grasping at straws, yet when one is drowning, it is the last vestige of hope. All right, Therese, in the absence of anything more tangible, we will grasp your straws and guard your penny candle.

Ilse: Are you forgetting that no light whatsoever is permissible in the barracks after midnight under pain of death?

Helena: But who will see it on a night like this. All the guards stay indoors except those in the watchtowers and luckily, our barracks is at the furthest point from them.

Marysia: What about the Kapos? They patrol during the night and would welcome any opportunity to please their master by informing on us.

Therese: I will never understand how a fellow Jew can treat his companions with such sadistic cruelty. Yes, you are right, Marysia, especially that big Kapo, the one named Ivan the terrible and his mute companion Bruno Bettelheim. They would as soon kill us themselves rather than giving that pleasure to the SS.

Ilse: We will have to take it in turns to warn off the guards or the Kapos but I fear that that devil Freidrich will take a more unhealthy interest in Anna's state. I suspect that he feels deprived of her murder and will extract sadistic pleasure in observing first hand her suffering and pain. Mark my words; we have not heard the last of Hans Freidrich on this night.

Margot: According to the clock tower, it is now 11:00 pm so we have one more hour left. It is a very still night but I fear a storm is on the way, because I heard thunder in the distance and thought I saw flashes of lightning.

Marysia: Oh no, that's all we need now; your penny candle will be hard to be seen through a blizzard, Therese.

And speaking of candles, just how many do you have and where did you get them?

Therese: There are five candles and they were given to me by a very old rabbi. He said to me, "These are my sole possessions. The only things I could rescue when the Black Crows invaded our country. They have been blessed in our holy faith. May they bring light to the darkness which covers our lands. When I am gone, please say kiddush for me."

Five minutes later, he was waved to the right by the white glove of Dr Mengele and he entered the gas chambers.

Margot: Anna, you face a terrible ordeal but you have to be strong. Remember the last time we saw our family? You must, for their memory, choose to live; for sometimes, it takes more courage to live than to die.

Anna: I told you, Margot, that I am not afraid and I will reach out to your penny candle, Therese.

Therese: Good, now firstly, we must build up your strength and as the first resistance to cold is food, let us now gather our secret reserve and eat as much as possible.

Marysia: I have a strange feeling about this night but I agree with Therese so I suggest that we do eat as much as possible and worry about tomorrow when or if it comes.

Ilse: I agree, just imagine all the fine ladies on the Titanic who refused their desserts, worrying about their figures and for some of them, tomorrow did not come, so let's eat, drink and be merry.

Marysia: (Laughing) Don't finish that famous quotation just yet, Ilse, because tomorrow is coming from a place which does not yet exist. Let's see what surprises are in store for the inmates of Auschwitz/Birkenau.

Enter Henryk Goldszmit, aged 13

Henryk: Please, you must help me.

Marysia: Who are you and what do you want?

Henryk: My name is Henryk Goldszmit from Block 7. Please, you must help me. I need food

Marysia: So does everyone else in the camp. Why do you ask us for food, who sent you here?

Henryk: Nobody sent me, please, you must understand I don't want the food for me, it is for my friend Andrzej Stapor.

Ilse: How do we know that this is not some plan or trick to get us all in trouble? Let's see your arm quickly.

Henryk: (Showing tattoo) Please, you have to believe me. I know that you work in the reclaim section called 'Canada' and sometimes you get the food that is left behind by the prisoners when they are taken away.

Marysia: So, we give you some food and you go and tell others and then they will come, then more and more. We cannot take that risk.

Henryk: Please, I beg you, the food is not for me and if I am caught, I swear I will not tell anyone where I got it, on pain of death.

Therese: Where are you from, child, and who is this friend that you risk your life for?

Henryk: Andrzej and I are the sole survivors from the orphanage called Dom Sierot. When the Nazis came, they transferred all the orphans into the Jewish Ghetto in Warsaw. We would all have starved to death but for the actions of our Pan Doktor, or Mister Doctor as we called him. His name was Janusz Korczak.

Helena: You were one of Janus Korczak's orphans?

Therese: Who is Janus Korczak?

Helena: Janus Korczak is a legend in his own lifetime. He is a children's author and paediatrician and finally devoted his life working as a director of the orphanage in Warsaw.

Therese: But what became of him? (To Henryk) Did he come here with you?

Henryk: Yes, he came here with Andrzej and I and 194 other orphans.

Margot: Oh my God, you mean the entire orphanage was sent here to Auschwitz?

Henryk: Yes. He seemed to know what was going to happen to us all because in July, he decided that the children should put on a play called 'The Post Office'.

Therese: I know that play, it was written by Rabindranath Tagore and deals with the prospect of death.

Henryk: I think he wanted to prepare us in some way so as not to be afraid of the unknown.

Helena: Janus Korczak, he stayed with his children to the end.

Henryk: When the Germans came in August, I think it was the 5th or the 6th, it doesn't really matter, he gathered us all together and spoke very calmly about our excursion to the countryside, as he called it. I can still hear his words and feel the comfort of a promise of meadows of flowers, streams where we could bathe, woods full of bright-red berries and fields of mushrooms. We were then dressed in our very best clothes and marched two by two to the Umschlagplatz where we boarded the train to bring us here.

Ilse: So that was Janus Korczak. Oh dear God, I remember seeing the arrival of that train.

Anna: You were there, Ilse?

Ilse: Yes, I was there and I witnessed the most distressing scene ever imagined in depravity and hypocrisy. When the train came to a stop, all the doors were opened and the usual contents of humanity spilled out onto the platform. There were screams and shouts of both prisoners and guards and general milling of confused people. The very last cattle wagon was finally opened and one man alighted and proceeded to help his little charges down to the ground. Something strange then happened as a great hush descended on the entire station. This man, your Janusz Korczak, then took two little tots by the hand, they were aged three at most, and then started walking to the clump of trees beside the main crematorium at the furthest end of the track. The other children then followed, holding each other by the hand and each also carried a toy or a book. Every one of them was dressed in clean and meticulously cared-for clothes and each carried a blue knapsack.

Henryk: Like this one? (Producing a knapsack from under his shirt) Being one of the eldest at age 12, Andrzej and I were the last in the line. The youngest, aged three, were as you saw at the front with Pan Doctor.

Anna: Were the children not afraid, were they not crying?

Ilse: No, not a tear was shed. I think it was the serene dignity which shone on the faces of the orphans that stunned the other prisoners and even the guards into a respectful silence. Even the dogs lay down at their handler's feet as if they too were ashamed to be part of the coming murder of innocents. Not a sound was heard except the crunch of stones under the children's feet, which gradually faded as they approached the valley of the Birches beside the Crematorium. The last I saw of them was Janusz standing at the doorway, talking calmly to the children as they entered the chamber of death.

Margot: Did no one offer a protest; was there no pity or mercy shown?

Ilse: Protest, Pity, Mercy, these are mere words that have no meaning here, no, once the children had passed from sight, a terrible reality returned that even GOD Himself was powerless to intervene.

Anna: You said that your Pan Doktor, Janusz, was able to save you and your friend. Did he himself survive or any other of the children?

Henryk: When we entered the dressing rooms, an SS man recognised Janusz as being the author of one of his children's favourite storybook and offered to give

Janusz his freedom. Pan Doktor looked at him then looked at the children whom he cared for and said, "I cannot and will not abandon my children." It was then that Janusz saw a chance that Andrzej and I might escape and his plan worked perfectly. He noticed a sweeping brush and a mop lying against the walls of the dressing rooms and told us to start sweeping and cleaning the floor. We had already taken off the top part of our uniform so we did not now look like the other orphans who entered the chamber. The last time I saw Pan Doktor was when the steel doors of the Gas chamber closed on him and 192 of my young brothers and sisters of the Dom Sierot Orphanage. We then finished our cleaning tasks and walked brazenly past the two guards at the door who scarcely gave us a glance. Both of us then joined another working party where we have survived until now.

Margot: What a courageous and brave man to decline his own freedom to stay with his children. No greater love has man than he should lay down his life for his friends.

Therese: And what better way to honour such bravery is to help his only survivors to live to testify to such courage and loyalty.

Henryk: I would dearly love to quote his favourite words on a monument to his unselfish live. He often said and his words will be forever ingrained in my memory, "Even the darkest days and nights can never last when the spark of Hope ignites a new beginning. Hope is a trust that life is good and Love is powerful."

Therese: Two daring young children who have survived with Hope as their emblem. Yes, Henryk, we will do everything in our power to help you and your friend Andrzej.

Margot: What illness has befallen Andrzej that makes you risk the long trek from Block 7 to our Quarters?

Henryk: Last week Andrzej appeared at roll call without his cap. Someone stole it from him while he slept and by then it was too late to try to find a replacement.

Therese: Oh my God, that is an offence that merits a death sentence.

Henryk: We both knew that but we could only hope that the Kapo would not notice it in the dark.

Ilse: No such luck. I really believe that some of those Kapos deliberately steal caps from the sleeping prisoners so that they can enjoy the execution.

Henryk: Yes, it was the big Kapo, Bruno Bettelheim, you know, the one they call Ivan the Terrible, who dragged Andrzej out in front of the SS man. There were three other prisoners also caught for the same offence so the four of them were brought before that SS sadist Freidrich.

Marysia: Yes, sadist is the right word to describe that evil person. But if Freidrich was in charge, how is it that your friend still lives?

Henryk: By the grace of God, Andrzej survived but only when Freidrich's gun jammed when he calmly shot the first three in the head. The Kapo then stepped forward and offered to bludgeon Andrzej to death as a lesson to the other prisoners. Freidrich, however, delayed for a moment and I thought that he would show some mercy in recognition of such providence. But he just smiled as he addressed the assembled prisoners and said, "The prisoner has survived an execution which he truly deserves but let us now see just how much longer he will survive secure in the knowledge that no hand will be raised against him. I now sentence the prisoner to a long life or should I say as long as he will last without food or water. Take him away." Andrzej has now been in Block 12 for the past 8 days with ten other prisoners including my other friend a Polish priest called Fr. Maximilian Kolbe.

Anna: I too am to suffer punishment under SS man Freidrich but it is nothing to the terrible torture endured by your friend. Please take whatever food you need but I am very much afraid that if you are caught trying to smuggle anything into those poor victims, then your own fate will be even worse.

Henryk: I am willing to take that chance because I know that Andrzej would do the same for me, and so would Janusz Korczak.

Margot: We will fill your blue knapsack with as much food as you can carry and as Anna says, please be very careful. I am sure Freidrich will hope for such a rescue attempt and it will give him great pleasure in inflicting more torture to any rescuer.

Girls, now fill his knapsack with bits of bread and sausage.

Therese: We will include you in our prayers tonight and hope that God will look down favourably on both you and Anna. Now may God go with you and may we all meet again when this madness finally ends.

Exit Henryk
End Act 1, Scene 2

Act 11

Marysia: Well, that's all our secret food reserves eaten and we still have half an hour before those swine return.

Therese: That is our physical needs attended to, now we must prepare mentally with emphasis on the positive power of thinking.

Ilse: For what it's worth, Anna, we gypsies are probably more used to the cold and how to survive in harsh conditions than most other people. You have to use the conditions to benefit yourself. The snow outside is about a foot deep at the moment so try to use that snow as a blanket around your exposed feet. It will help to reduce the wind chill, which is the most dangerous part of your ordeal.

Margot: Seeing as they are making her stand barefoot, will they allow her extra bodily clothes?

Marysia: I wouldn't depend on it if Freidrich turns up. He might insist on her wearing the threadbare grey dresses of the normal prisoners, but we do have that singular privilege of wearing our own clothes and if so, let's try to make her look as inconspicuous as possible with as much underclothes as possible.

Anna: I am so sorry and feel very guilty for putting you to all this trouble. I don't want any of you to risk any punishment on my behalf; after all, it was my fault alone for not sorting those last three suitcases before the Kapo arrived.

Margot: You're just lucky that Bruno did not simply beat you to death there and then. But if you remember, his partner Leopold did try to make little of it until the other SS guard arrived.

Marysia: You are right on both counts, Margot, because whatever compassion is left in those Kapos, only Leopold Kowsky retains any resemblance of a conscience. The other brute, Bruno Bettelheim is just a dumb sadist whose powerful build and small brain is just what the SS need to enforce order by sheer terror.

Helena: You seem to know a lot about our captors, I mean you know their names and where they are from.

Marysia: That's right, Helena. I know most of them and those I don't know I try to learn more about them. There is a method in my madness and my memory of names and faces will ensure some form of retribution when this war ends and these people will face a universal justice.

Helena: And what if the war does not end or the Germans gain total victory, what then, what other possible future is in store for the world?

Ilse: This war was has been raging since Sept 1939 and it is now Jan 1945. The tide of war has turned against the Germans so there is no question of a Nazi victory. Peace will return – I am sure of it – and I feel it will be sooner rather than later.

Margot: I hope you are right, Ilse. This nightmare seems never ending ever since our capture and I am sure that everyone has experienced the same terror in every country the Nazi's have invaded.

Therese: Their obsession to rid the world of Judaism even extended to what I considered to be a safe haven. Three of us lived on Guernsey in the Channel Islands and felt secure and confident that it would be too much bother or trouble for the Nazis to take notice of a few solitary Jewish workers. It was not to be, however, and we were forced to report for deportation to France and then a one-way ticket to Auschwitz.

Margot: Did no one stand up for you or try to help you or even hide you from the Nazis?

Therese: The three of us, Marianne Grunfeld, Auguste Spitz and myself had fled our homelands of Austria and Poland to escape the purge of anti-Semitism. We begged the Guernsey authorities to protest strongly against our deportation, assuring those same authorities that their compliance with the Nazis would end in certain death for us all. No protest was made on our behalf and upon our arrival here, my two companions were sent direct to the crematorium. Even a single voice of protest would have registered as a proud moment in the history of Guernsey; instead, this one instance will forever leave an indelible stain on the islands past.

Margot: And yet even after such betrayal, you are willing to help Anna.

Therese: My two friends are gone but for the wave of one gloved hand to the right, I am still alive, and I will be proud to help Anna and you in any way I can.

Ilse: It was the same for me. You know, I think I was left alive for a purpose, not only for remembering our Holy people, but also that this never happens again in humanity. We arrived at the train station in Lodz and the cattle cars were wide open. We weren't given a ramp like animals do, no; we were just taken like pieces of garbage and thrown into the cattle cars. Under these terrible conditions, we travelled without food or sanitation for three days and three nights until the train eventually stopped in the middle of the night. The doors were then unlocked and men in striped suits came at us and started throwing us out. They said to us, "Don't take anything, you'll get it later. If somebody falls down, you are not allowed to pick them up; the same applies to children. You just have to go on."

And then the yelling starts: "Women on one side with the children, men on the other side, five in a row, now, go, run, fast."

And all the time, this is accompanied by yelling, beating, shooting and being torn apart by the dogs. We arrived in one place where there was a group of SS. Among them is Mengele, who did the selections with his white gloves and his finger going right or left. We have no idea what this means, right or left and when our family arrived with this group, we were told to stop. From the whole family, I am the 16-year-old who is thrown to the right, obviously, I looked strong enough to work. When they separated us, the people who went to the left were taken straight to the crematorium. My mother looked back at me and although I could not hear her above the screaming, her lips said, "Live for us."

That was the last time I ever saw a member of my family.

We were taken to the right into a room and told to undress. There were little stools lined up against the wall and we were told to sit facing the wall. From the back, they came and shaved all our hair, all parts of the body and there we remained like shorn sheep. They took away everything from us, family pictures, clothes, glasses, jewellery, and if you can't take off your earrings fast enough, they cut them off. We were then marched outside and we looked at each other and cannot recognise each other. Nobody recognises each other, even sisters, and everybody is given that grey dress. Suddenly, we realise these are girls from Ukraine, Poland and Czechoslovakia, who are suffering there. And we ask them when are we going to see our family again and they said to me, "Stupid Hungarian, don't you know where you are, don't you know you are in Auschwitz, don't you know what Auschwitz is, don't you see the chimney, don't you see the fire jumping out of it? That's where they're burning your people now."

And I fell back in fear and terror and shock and disbelief and then the full reality of my mother's last request that I should live gave me that strength to cope with this living hell.

Margot: All your personal accounts echo the same sense of loss, betrayal and suffering endured by the inmates of these Concentration camps. Both Anna and I are under no false illusions as to our eventual fate. Yet, I feel that if we endure and survive this night in particular, then our salvation might be nearer than we can imagine.

Anna: Margot is right, because I too feel a sense of liberation or freedom, which I know will help me to endure this coming ordeal.

Therese: You are a very brave girl, Anna, and like Ilse and Marysia, you MUST live to bear witness to the fate of your families and ensure their precious memories are enshrined in a monument that will bear testament to the most inglorious and despicable chapter in the history of humanity.

Anna: Margot and I are the sole survivors of a divided family, a family torn apart by prejudice and anti-Semitism. Our mother died when I was one years old and my father, even then, was ostracised on account of his Jewish faith. Three years later, our two older brothers were taken from us and sent separately to live with a true Aryan family whose duty was to re-educate them into a new religion and a new resurgent Germany. Both Margot and I were to remain with our father to eke out an existence, which slowly but surely took its toll on his already poor health. When he died, we were literally rescued from the streets by our Jewish neighbours only to succumb to the mass round-ups of all Jews, which eventually delivered us here to our fate.

Margot: If only our two brothers had remained with us, things may have turned out differently, but the only memory we still have of a once-happy family is this old photograph taken in 1932.

Therese: Margot, such possessions carry an immediate death sentence, please be careful.

Margot: I am aware of the risk but I have always protected and kept it well hidden in the hope that one day we might all meet again, whether it is on Earth or in Heaven.

Look, there's Momma holding Anna in her arms, and Poppa holding me. There's Karl, the eldest aged ten and Walther next aged eight. One frozen moment in time and yet, more precious than all the gold in the world, for this photograph contains a lifetime of happiness.

Therese: What became of your brothers or did you try to find them?

Anna: Since our rescue from the streets, we had moved through many towns and cities but all attempts by us to trace our brothers were thwarted by uncaring authorities and red tape. I am sure that any search by our brothers for us would be equally futile.

I was only three years old when I saw them last but still remember my Karly and Walty like it was yesterday.

Margot: We can only hope and pray that, somehow, they will survive this war or perhaps even now they too are also under sentence of death Hitler's other death camps.

Marysia: Face the truth, girls: if they have been Re-Germanised or in reality, brainwashed, they are now Hitler's most loyal followers with no memory of their religion or morality. Anyway, we have more urgent matters to attend to here and what worries me is that the thunderstorm is getting closer.

Therese: Do you think the SS men will come to supervise the punishment personally or will they leave it to the Kapos?

Marysia: You can bet that Hans Freidrich will not want to miss his sadistic party and will more likely wish to witness Anna's suffering first hand.

Helena: But even he will not stand around in freezing conditions for such a long time from midnight to first roll call.

Ilse: That's what I am afraid of, you see, when he tires or becomes bored witnessing her suffering, he may wish to personally end his amusement by doing what he does best: execution.

Margot: No, we cannot allow that to happen, not to Anna.

Anna: Margot, if that is what happens, you must not say or do anything; otherwise, he will execute everyone and as Ilse says, if even only one of us survive then that person is a witness for humanity. Nothing else matters as long as the world does not forget this, this Holocaust.

Therese: Holocaust, Holocaust, Anna, that is the one single word that truly describes this unspeakable, barbaric treatment of human beings.

Helena: Let us not speak any more about death or executions or what may happen in the near future. Remember, the future is coming from a place which does not yet exist, it passes through that which cannot be measured and it goes to a place which no longer exists.

Ilse: You're right, Helena, but only to a degree. Yes, the future does not yet exist, and only a Psychic or a damn fool would dare to predict it, but only a bigger fool would disregard it and not take precautions against whatever darker part of that future is yet to unfold.

Margot: You mean, of course, SS man Hans Freidrich.

Ilse: Yes, I firmly believe that Freidrich is a spawn of evil incarnate and if I know or suspect that his immediate intentions are the murder of any one of us, then I will not die like a lamb to the slaughter.

Therese: What can you do, what can any one of us do to fight this man and his fellow devils?

Ilse: Perhaps I can do very little, yet even if I spit in his face before his bullets kill me I will die with a smile on my face. Let us not forget that there is strength and unity in numbers so why not let that unity become our sole weapon.

Marysia: If it comes down to a physical defence of our lives, there is, I agree, a greater chance of survival by standing together as in 'one for all and all for one'. We don't have guns or knives or spears but we might have surprise on our side, together with other weapons.

Ilse: Other weapons, like what?

Marysia: Like this poker, a pot of boiling water, stones, timber, and don't forget that your fingers can tear out eyes. Those weapons.

Therese: And even if we subdue one or two of these people, what then? Where do we go? What do we do?

Marysia: As Helena says, there is no future, no tomorrow, only a present and at present, we are still alive. My one dream, which still keeps me alive, is to testify to the world that this Holocaust did happen and to personally face Hans Freidrich on an equal footing or take him with me in death.

Margot: It is getting near the time of Anna's punishment so let's forget, for the moment, dreams of revenge and prepare a way for Anna to survive this ordeal.

Ilse: Remember, Anna, the snow will protect you from the worst of the cold frost so keep looking at your penny candle and think of its warmth and light. Try to remember happier times with your family and live in the hope that you will meet them all again. I know that you are afraid but fear cannot be without some hope, nor hope without some fear.

Helena: Hope,that is the one word which utterly defeats despair, so grab hold of it and don't let go. You know, my mother used to sing a song to me many years ago, although I only remember the refrain. It was: (singing)
Whispering hope,
Oh, how welcome thy voice,
Making my heart
In its sorrow rejoice.

Marysia: Soft as the voice of an angel
Breathing a lesson unheard
Hope with a gentle persuasion
Whispers her comforting word
Wait, till the darkness is over
Wait, till the tempest is done
Hope for the sunshine tomorrow
After the shower is gone

(Therese and Helena join in):
Whispering hope
Oh, how welcome thy voice
Making my heart
In its sorrow rejoice

Marysia: If, in the dusk of the twilight
Dim be the region afar
Will not the deepening darkness
Brighten the glimmering star?
Then when the night is upon us
Why should the heart sink away?
When the dark midnight is over
Watch for the breaking of day.

All: Whispering hope,
Oh, how welcome thy voice
Making my heart

DOOR CRASHES OPEN.
ENTER HANS AND TWO KAPOS.

Hans: Well, well, well, a private party, and I wasn't even invited.

(To Helena) What say you, bitch??

Helena: We are very sorry if we have offended you, Herr Commander, we meant no harm.

Hans: You have offended me, you offend me every day that you live. I have more time and respect for the lice and vermin that infest this camp than you sub-human animals. It will give me the greatest pleasure to see you all die as quickly as possible and your filthy race finally cleansed by fire.

(To Anna) What say you, bitch? Do I speak the truth?

Anna: If it pleases you, Herr Commander, our lives are in your hands and we are grateful to you for our very existence. We beg you for mercy.

Hans: We beg you for mercy, we beg you for mercy. I hear those exact same words every day. Even in the last half hour, one of your kind begged for mercy yet strangely not for himself but for his poor, poor friend. He was carrying a knapsack full of bread and I wondered just where exactly did he get this contraband at this time of night?

(He signals to Kapo who throws a blood-stained blue knapsack on ground)

Anna: Oh dear God.

Hans: It appears that you recognise this knapsack!

(To Kapos) It seems our search for the collaborators is over. What say you, bitch, do you admit your guilt?

Anna: If it pleases you, Herr Commander, yes, I do recognise this knapsack or one like it. We were all given one of these each when we left our Orphanage in Warsaw to come here. I have not seen one like it until this very moment and was shocked only by the memory of it.

Hans: You expect me to believe such a story.

Margot: It is the truth, Herr Commander. We all had one just like that one but they were all taken from us when we arrived here.

Hans: Give me the names of anyone else who owned one of these knapsacks.

Margot: We had no names, Herr Commander, except pet names for our closest friends but none of them have survived since we came here.

Hans: When we capture this boy, and I assure you he will be captured, he will be brought here and if I find that he obtained his contraband from this section, then you will all suffer the same fate as his friend.

Therese: Herr Commander, what exactly did this boy do to implicate us in such an accusation to our section and was he not captured at the scene of his crime?

Hans: He tried to smuggle food through a ground window in Block 12 but was caught in the act by the Kapos. It was when he started begging for mercy for his friend that this fool of a Kapo. (Indicates Bruno) let him slip out of his prison shirt and he ran off into the night.

Anna: He begged for mercy not for himself but for his friend? Herr Commander, we also beg you for mercy for that boy and his friend. We beg you for mercy for us and to forgive us for the way God created us in our own imperfections.

Hans: There is no place for imperfection in the Third Reich, and there is only one true God, one Fuhrer, and His name is Adolf Hitler.

Helena: That is blasphemous.

Hans: You dare to belittle my God in my presence? Well, now, let's see whose God is more powerful.
You and you (Anna and Helena) kneel!

Therese: Please, Herr Commander, have mercy, they didn't mean any insult or affront.

Hans: Shut up, slut!

(To Kapos) If any one of them speaks another word, beat them to death.

Now, let us see whose God is more powerful. I am now going to count to ten, at the end of which I will shoot both of you. If your God is more powerful than my finger, then He will stop me from pulling the trigger. If not, it will prove that the Aryan God is the one true God whom we should all serve faithfully. Well, do you both accept the challenge on behalf of Jehovah, or are you both scared of meeting Him so soon? Or maybe, in your case, Hell is more fitting for your race.

Helena: We do not lack courage, Herr Commander, but yes, we are scared, yet there can be no courage unless you are scared, because courage is being afraid but going on anyhow. Anna is 12 years of age and has suffered grievously under Nazi rule, but it is better to suffer wrong than to do it. For this reason, our last words on this earth are that before God, we are equally wise and equally foolish and remember that the acts of this life are the destiny of the next. Look to yourself, Commander, we forgive you and all who have offended us, not for you, but for ourselves.

Hans: My one failing in this life is my generosity in allowing you extra minutes of life, but I will extend this generosity in allowing ONE of you to live, to die another day. I will now start to count to ten. The first of you to cry for mercy will be spared and one of you can then watch the other die. In this way, either one of you will decide the fate of the other. The first to cry mercy will in fact be pulling the trigger on the other. If no voice is raised, you both die. Now, let us put your God to the test.

EINS ZWEI DREI VIER FUNF SECHS SIEBEN ACHT NEUN

(During the count, the gun is pointed at each girl in turn, starting with Anna)
DOOR BURSTS OPEN. ENTER FRANZ

Franz: What is going on here?

Hans: (To girls) It appears your God has arrived at the last moment to rescue you, but don't worry, the respite will be short lived. Forgive me, Franz, but your visit is ill timed or appropriate, depending on the point of view. I was about to dispense justice in a very amusing way but your arrival has deprived me of my bit of fun.

Franz: Your bit of fun may be interrupted more seriously by the arrival of something more sinister and threatening than my good self.

Hans: What are you talking about?

Franz: The storm clouds are gathering outside but it is not thunder you hear, but Russian guns. (To Kapos) You two, report to the commandant's office and prepare for evacuation.

Hans: What about these prisoners?

Franz: All prisoners will be transported to the Fatherland

Hans: How much time do we have before the arrival of the Russians?

Franz: A day, maybe two at the most.

Hans: A day, at least, well, now, all I need is a few hours to dispense some good German justice.

Franz: Are you mad, do you not fear Russian retribution? Our orders are to destroy, where possible, all evidence of our activities. The sappers have already laid explosives in Crematorium 1 and 2. They will detonate them at midnight. All stocks of Zyklon B have been shipped to Jasenovac and Dachau.

Hans: (To girls) Don't think for a moment that deliverance is at hand. You may have escaped the Gas chambers and the chimneys for now, but you have not escaped death.

Look at me, look into my eyes. The eyes they say are the mirrors of the soul but what you will see there is death. I am Death.

Franz: We have done our duty to the Fuhrer and now we must face the reality and consequences of our actions. Hans, I ask you to put aside this madness and look to our own futures, and maybe salvage some honour from this situation.

Hans: Honour, honour, must I remind you of your oath? "My honour lies in loyalty."

No, this scum will die tonight.

(To Anna) You, your God here (Franz) saved you the last time but now you will most surely die. Any last words to your friends, and if so, you will speak to them directly to the barrel of my gun. When I tire of your drivel, I will silence you forever.

Anna: I ask you for mercy, Herr Commander; let your heart guide you in what you must do, it whispers, so listen carefully. I proudly wear and bear the Star of David and honour the memory of Momma and Poppa. I will soon be in their company once again and will ask my God to protect my sister from this fate I must suffer. You are impatient for this sacrifice, Herr Commander, but I ask you to allow my last breath to whisper the names of my two darling brothers who were taken away from us by the madness of this war.

Karly and Walty, I love you.

Hans: (Visibly shaken and bewildered)

Karly and Walty, *Nein, Nein,* this is wrong.

Your time has come, Jew.

Franz: Put down your gun, Hans.

Hans: *Nein, Nein,* these Jews will be executed.

Franz: What do those names – Karly and Walty – mean to you? Has it stirred a memory of a past life?

Hans: Those names mean nothing to me; this little bitch has bewitched me and distracted me from my duty, now no more talk.

Franz: (Aiming gun at Hans) Put down your gun, Hans.

Hans: Are you insane? Threatening a fellow officer will have you in front of a firing squad!

Franz: I have no wish to kill you but I will do so unless I have time to question the prisoner. Now, give me your gun.

(Hans does so)

(Franz raises Anna from her kneeling posture)

I remember the name Anna many lifetimes ago. I also remember the names Karly and Walty. The names come from somewhere in my mind that suggest a previous existence, a *déjà vu* and yet a paradox. An impossibility and yet, a twist of fate, I am confused.

(To Hans) You also recognised the names Karly and Walty so how do you explain this mystery?

Hans: There is no mystery. I have been raised as a true Aryan, and if there is confusion, it is the fault of these Jewish bitches who have somehow bewitched us.

Yes, that's it; they both have cast a spell over us to extend their miserable lives. I have never heard the names Anna or Margot before.

Franz: How did you know her sister's name is Margot?

Hans: Someone must have said her name

Anna: (Taking out her locket)

If it please you, Herr Commander, I know I should not have this locket, but I have kept it safe and hidden and guarded it with my life at stake.

This is my family.

Franz: (Puts Hans' gun on the table and takes the locket) Oh my dear God, This can't be true, Hans, look!

Hans: *Nein, Nein*, this is witchcraft, this is a fake. This is a filthy Jewish trick to deceive us. I am not a Filthy Jew.

Franz: You cannot deny the reality and truth of this picture. I too find this incredible but the reality of the situation, distasteful as it may be to our ingrained culture, compels us to accept our true identity and destiny. I do remember the name Karl and I remember the name Walther, your name Hans or should I say Walty, my brother.

Hans: *Nein*, I am not a Jew, I am a true Aryan. I do not know these people, I do not know you, I do not want to know you and I would rather die first.

Anna: (To Hans) Herr Commander, I am sorry for what I am and I am sorry for what you have become. There is something happening here tonight that is very powerful and there is an emotion that is desperately trying to surface from its burial place behind these barbwire fences. It is LOVE.

Franz: Anna, Margot, I am your Karly.
(All embrace)

Marysia: (Now with other gun)
(To Franz) Herr Commander, place your gun on the table. Please do not underestimate my proficiency with a gun and I am fully prepared to use it to dispense good old Jewish justice

Margot: Marysia, what are you doing? The danger is past us, my brothers can help us now.

Marysia: The Leopard never changes his spots, this one (Karly) may have seen the light, but this one (Walty) is evil incarnate and whatever semblance or spark of humanity that may have once existed there is forever extinguished. No, this one is going to answer tonight for the crimes of his nation against humanity.

Therese: No, Marysia, it is not up to you to dispense justice. Maybe he does deserve to die, but if it is by your hand then you will become the very same killer that you despise.

Anna: Whoever saves one life, saves the entire world, please, Marysia, has there not been enough killing and suffering?

Helena: Marysia, the last words of our Saviour after suffering the most hideous torture was, "Father, forgive them for they know not what they do."

Marysia: (Still pointing the gun at Hans) What say you, Commander? Do you fear death? You, who has dispensed death so easily on a daily basis? Are you ready to come face to face with your victims? To tell them why you turned a deaf ear to their cries of pain? To deny them the smallest act of mercy?

Hans: I am a soldier, a loyal soldier of the Third Reich and I was obliged to follow orders.

Marysia: Following orders, only following orders. Is this to be the catchphrase of your Nazi regime, does this exonerate you and your kind from any personal blame or responsibility for your genocide? How could you not be moved by the tears and cries of the 1000 children whom you fed into the Crematoriums on a daily basis, seven days a week, every week for the past three years? But of course, they were not children; they were human animals whom you burned, drowned, strangled, tortured and slaughtered. Who speaks for them now? I have waited and prayed for this moment for a long time. Look at me, Commander, look at me and die.

Hans: You don't understand; the Jewish race is responsible for all the evils that befell our country. International Jewry is the cancer of the entire human race and its poisonous influence had to be stopped and totally eradicated. The world should be thanking us for our actions.

Anna: (Goes to Hans) Herr Commander, Walty, you are my brother, you were born a Jew and no denial can change that, please don't deny or condemn our holy nation which gave birth to you.

Marysia: Enough of this drivel, Herr Commander. I am a Jew, in your eyes, a filthy Jew. You came here tonight to administer a sadistic punishment to a 12-year-old girl.

I have witnessed your depravity over the years and tonight, but for the grace of God, you would have cheerfully sent your own sister to her death. You don't deserve to have a family, you who has destroyed so many in the past, yet tonight, a greater power has intervened, a power which I will not contest or judge. Vengeance is mine, sayeth The Lord, I bow to His judgement.

(She lowers the gun)

Hans: (Grabbing Anna and producing a knife, which he holds to Anna's neck)

Drop that gun, bitch, or your little friend here dies now! Do it or I swear this room will run red with blood.

Franz: Hans, you do not mean that. Anna is your sister.

Hans: I have no sisters or brothers here, my real brothers and sisters are in the SS.

And you have betrayed the sacred oath you took to the Fatherland, 'My honour lies in loyalty.' (He spits) You will wear those words around your neck when you face a firing squad, which I will happily command. Now, for the last time, put the gun on the floor or this bitch dies right now.

(Marysia does so) Now kick it over here.

(She does so)

(As Hans goes down to pick it up, Anna runs back to others, Franz has now retrieved his own gun from the table and points it at Hans)

Franz: There will be no more killing, Hans. The war is over, we will have to answer for the crimes of our nation, please put down the gun.

Hans: What's one more killing out of six million?

Franz: What madness are you saying, six million who?

Hans: I saw the combined death toll from all our concentration camps throughout Europe, and they now total over six million Jews. So, a handful more will not make a great difference. Now, no more talk, its either you or them.

Franz: No!

(Both shoot and blackout)
(Lights up on both men lying dead)
(Enter two Russian soldiers, one makes the announcement)

Soldiers: YOU HAVE ALL BEEN LIBERATED BY THE FORCES OF THE SOVIET SOCIALIST REPUBLIC THE WAR IS OVER

(All gather round the two bodies as Anna cradles Walty and Margot cradles Karly)

Whispering Hope is sung by Olive Kline and Elsie Baker. (Recorded in 1914, complete with old time scratchy phonograph recording)

During this song, Henryk enters, supporting his very sick but still-living friend Andrzej.

Marysia then lifts Anna while Therese lifts Margot and all exit, leaving Karly and Walty on floor. They exit into a very bright light, leaving spotlights on Karly and Walty, which gradually fades with the end of the music into total darkness on the stage but a white light remains at the exit.

Fade at the end of music

The End

I visited Auschwitz in April 2009 and walked beneath the same imposing gates that welcomed the millions of innocent men, women and children to their doom nearly 70 years ago. One thousand children were herded like cattle on a daily basis into the gas chambers, where they suffered an excruciating, slow, painful death by the inhalation of crystallised prussic acid or more infamously known as Zyklon B.

This process continued unabated, day in day out, until the Crematoriums were blown up by the Nazis themselves on 27 January 1945 in an attempt to obliterate their dreadful crimes against humanity.

Since that time, various ludicrous claims that the Holocaust was a myth have been propounded by irresponsible organisations and even religions whose motives are as despicable as the crimes they try to cover up in their ignorance and intolerance.

We should never forget the suffering of the inmates of all the concentration camps during World War II but especially the Jewish Nation who were singled out for 'Special Treatment'.

The Jewish Nation's contribution to the culture and well-being of the world is easily recognised by their accumulation of Nobel Prizes in Literature, Peace, Physics, Economics and Medicine.

'Anna – The Girl Who Stood Out in the Cold' is based on a true event, yet sadly is only one out of the six million other personal stories that will never be told.

The comment of one survivor of Auschwitz, 70 years after liberation, speaks volumes in its simplicity, "The lips may smile, but the heart still weeps."

The monument in Birkenau states: FOREVER LET THIS PLACE BE A CRY OF DESPAIR AND A WARNING TO HUMANITY. WHERE THE NAZIS MURDERED ABOUT ONE AND A HALF MILLION MEN, WOMEN AND CHILDREN. MAINLY JEWS FROM VARIOUS COUNTRIES OF EUROPE.
AUSCHWITZ – BIRKENAU
1940–1945

'Anna – The Girl Who Stood Out in the Cold' tells the story of 12-year-old Anna Kersten, who was sentenced to stand outside in her bare feet throughout a Polish winter's night whose temperatures drop as low as 30 °C.. This was a sentence imposed on her by a brutal SS prison guard as punishment for not reaching her daily work quota in the infamous Auschwitz Concentration Camp.

Her other fellow inmates contrived to help her to survive this ordeal. However, it is not just the freezing temperatures they have to contend with but a more sinister threat from the sadistic SS officer, Hans Freidrich, intent on ensuring the punishment is carried through to its dreadful conclusion.